Catch the Baby!

Catch the Baby!

Story by Lee Kingman

Pictures by Susanna Natti

Puffin Books

PUFFIN BOOKS
Published by the Penguin Group
Penguin Books USA Inc., 375 Hudson Street, New York, New York 10014, U.S.A.
Penguin Books Ltd, 27 Wrights Lane, London W8 5TZ, England
Penguin Books Australia Ltd, Ringwood, Victoria, Australia
Penguin Books Canada Ltd, 10 Alcorn Avenue, Toronto, Ontario, Canada M4V 3B2
Penguin Books (N.Z.) Ltd, 182–190 Wairau Road, Auckland 10, New Zealand

Penguin Books Ltd, Registered Offices: Harmondsworth, Middlesex, England

First published in the United States of America by Viking Penguin,
a division of Penguin Books USA Inc., 1990
Published in Puffin Books, 1993

10 9 8 7 6 5 4 3 2 1

LIBRARY OF CONGRESS CATALOGING-IN-PUBLICATION DATA
Kingman, Lee.
    Catch the baby! / story by Lee Kingman;
pictures by Susanna Natti.   p.   cm.
    "First published in the United States of America by Viking Penguin, a
division of Penguin Books USA Inc., 1990"—T.p. verso.
    Summary: A rambunctious toddler, eager to explore, leads her
brother and sister on a merry romp through the fields surrounding
their home.
    ISBN 0-14-050762-0
    [1. Play—Fiction.   2. Stories in rhyme.]   I. Natti, Susanna,
ill.   II. Title.
[PZ8.3.K614Cat   1993]   [E]—dc20   92-26588

Printed in the United States of America
Set in Clearface

With thanks for inspiration
over the years
to Lisl Weil
and thanks to our own
lively models
Lydia and Kate Willsky

Catch the baby! She's running out
to see what all the world's about.

Oh, catch the baby! Hurry up!

before she picks that buttercup,

before she reaches out to pat

the fuzzy lazy snoozy cat.

Oh, stop the baby! Do it quick
before she tries to snatch that stick
away from Woofer. Look around—

what is she watching on the ground?

Perhaps she wants to take a jog
and jump! jump! like a jouncy frog.

Look! Now she's running off the path

to join the robin in his bath.

She's out of sight. Where has she gone?
Wait! There she is across the lawn.

She's making this into a chase.
Look at the grin there on her face.

What has she found behind those flowers?

Poor Teddy! He's been lost for hours.

Can you see now who she's greeting?

It's a big bug. *Not for eating!*

Now look at what she wants to try—
oh, catch the baby! That's too high!

Quick! Pick her up and clean her face

and tie her ribbon back in place.

So here we are, all safe and snug—
all ready for our Mama's hug.